Johnny

JOHNNY CROW'S PARTY

Johnny Crow's Party

Tea in the Garden.

WARNE CLASSICS SERIES

Illustrated by Randolph Caldecott:

A FIRST CALDECOTT COLLECTION
The House that Jack Built • A Frog He Would a-Wooing Go

A SECOND CALDECOTT COLLECTION
Sing a Song for Sixpence • The Three Jovial Huntsmen

A THIRD CALDECOTT COLLECTION
The Queen of Hearts • The Farmer's Boy

Written and illustrated by L. Leslie Brooke:

JOHNNY CROW'S GARDEN
JOHNNY CROW'S PARTY
JOHNNY CROW'S NEW GARDEN

JOHNNY CROW'S PARTY

L. LESLIE BROOKE

FREDERICK WARNE

FREDERICK WARNE

Penguin Books Ltd, Harmondsworth, Middlesex, England
Viking Penguin Inc., 40 West 23rd Street, New York, New York 10010, U.S.A.
Penguin Books Australia Ltd, Ringwood, Victoria, Australia
Penguin Books Canada Limited, 2801 John Street, Markham, Ontario, Canada L3R 1B4

First published 1907
Reprinted 1910, 1912, 1916, 1920, 1922, 1924, 1925,
1926, 1927, 1928, 1929, 1930, 1932, 1935, 1938,
1941, 1942, 1946, 1947, 1949, 1951,
1956, 1959, 1962 and 1966

This re-set edition published 1986
Copyright © Frederick Warne & Co., 1907, 1986
All rights reserved. Without limiting the rights under copyright reserved above, no part of this publication may be reproduced, stored in or introduced into a retrieval system, or transmitted, in any form or by any means (electronic, mechanical, photocopying, recording or otherwise), without the prior written permission of the copyright owner.

ISBN 0 7232 3428 0

Typeset by CCC, printed and bound in Great Britain by
William Clowes Limited, Beccles and London

TO MY NEPHEW
SOMERSET
HAPPY IN A NAME THAT
ASSURES HIS WELCOME
TO JOHNNY CROW'S – OR
ANY OTHER – PARTY

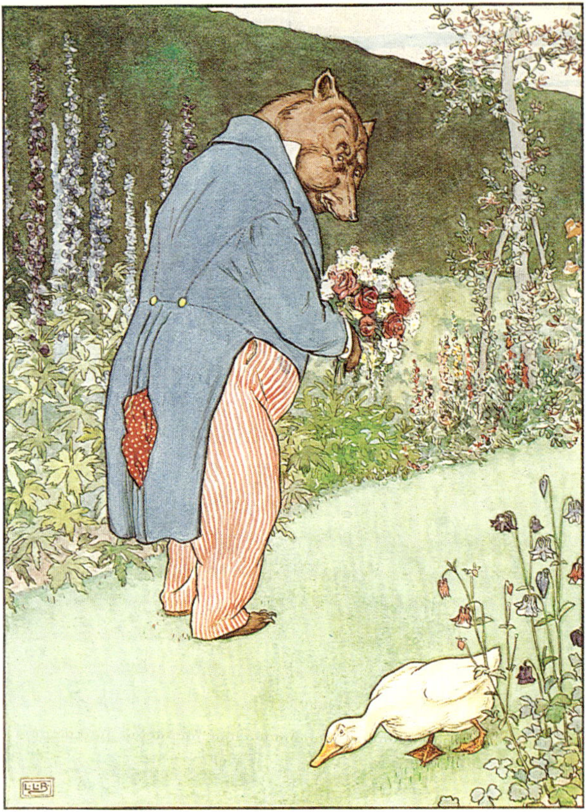

JOHNNY CROW'S PARTY

Johnny Crow
Plied Rake and Hoe

And improved his little Garden.

And the Eagle

Looked quite regal

In Johnny Crow's Garden.

And the Cockatoo
Said "*Comment vous portez vous?*"

And the Gander

Didn't understand her;

But the Flamingo
Talked the same lingo

In Johnny Crow's Garden.

And the Bear

Sang a sentimental Air,

But the Giraffe
Was inclined to laugh;

Even the Duckling
Couldn't help chuckling
In Johnny Crow's Garden.

Then the Snake

Got entangled with the rake

In Johnny Crow's Garden.

And the Cock

Had a very nasty knock;

So the Hen
Said:

"We'll never come again

To Johnny Crow's Garden!"

And the Sheep

Went to sleep,

And the Armadillo

Used him for a pillow;

And the Porcupine

Said: "Wake me if for talk you pine!"

In Johnny Crow's

Garden.

And the Kangaroo

Tried to paint the Roses blue

Till the Camel
Swallowed the Enamel,

And the Reindeer
Said: "I'm sorry for your pain, dear!"

In Johnny Crow's Garden.

So the Chimpanzee
Put the Kettle on for Tea;

And the Seal

Made a very big Meal;

While the Sole
Shared a Muffin with the Mole
In Johnny Crow's Garden.

Then they picked the Flowers, and
    wandered in the Maze,
And before they went their several ways

They all joined together
In a Hearty Vote of Praise

Of Johnny Crow and his

Garden.

Plan ✻ of ✻ the ✻ Maze ✻ in